DESIRING DARCY

COLLECTION

Carla Bency

BLURB

This collection features four erotic reimaginings for ODC. Mr. Darcy in moonlight entices Lizzy in one story. In another, they have a midnight liaison in the library that leads to much more than reading. Lizzy celebrates her first night as Darcy's bride in the third tale, and the last story is all about Lizzy's Desires.

TABLE OF CONTENTS

DARCY'S MIDNIGHT LIAISON

Blurb

When Lizzy has trouble sleeping at Netherfield, she seeks out the tried-and-true remedy of reading herself to sleep. She doesn't have the library to herself though. Mr. Darcy is there, and their usual quick wits and verbal sparring takes an unexpected turn as passions flare between them, and Darcy shows her a much more desirable way to prepare for sleep.

Lizzy found it difficult to sleep in a bed that was not her own, so she slipped from the room assigned to her, across the hall from where Jane laid abed in a Netherfield guestroom, regaining her strength. She paused long enough to crack the door to check on her sister.

The poor dear was snoring dreadfully and sounded woefully congested. Lizzy slipped inside to add a pillow behind her sister, which immediately improved her breathing. She still looked pale, with red patches on her cheeks, but she sounded better. Jane did not rouse during the process.

Once assured her sister was as comfortable as she could be under the circumstances, Lizzy took her leave. Her original destination had been the library, and she decided to continue onward to her destination. She drew her dressing gown even tighter around her and held up her candelabra as she moved through the house and downstairs to the library.

She breathed a sigh of contentment when she passed the doorway. Was there anything so pleasing as a library full of books? The smell was wondrous, and the idea of all the knowledge awaiting consumption filled her with giddiness. She knew others would laugh at her if she tried to explain how much she loved libraries, so she did not expound upon it. It was a secret…fetish.

She set the candelabra on a table nearby to free her hands. There was a plethora of choice at Netherfield, from the classics to more recent releases. She was browsing the newer treatises on women's rights when she heard the door click.

With a gasp, she looked up to see Darcy entering the room. He wore his dressing gown and a nightcap. It was quite intimate apparel, and she blushed as she looked away, conscious of wearing only three layers. Scandalous!

"Miss Bennet, pardon the intrusion. I saw a light and wondered which of my fellow insomniacs was perusing the stacks." He nodded his head.

She tried to quell the blush and nodded at him. "Prithee, do not let me disturb you, Mr. Darcy. I shall make a selection and leave you." She hastily grabbed a book, uncaring which one, or that it was dark enough in her chambers to make it difficult to read with just the one candelabra. She had to escape.

"Do not rush on my account, Miss Bennet." He came closer as he spoke, pausing only a few feet away. "I am not surprised to see you browsing that section."

She scowled at him. "Am I detecting condescension in your tone, sir?"

"Not at all. I have read many of them."

That did not seem like Darcy. "I see. How unexpected. Surely, you do not condone the half-dozen fine ladies of your acquaintance reading them though?"

His smile was enigmatic. "Perhaps not the finest of ladies, but I see no reason why you should not."

Lizzy's eyes narrowed. "I hardly know what to make of gaining your permission, if I desired it. One must surely see the insult in the statement."

Darcy quirked a brow. "Clarify, if you please, Miss Bennet. What insult?"

"You are surely implying I am no lady, so there is no harm in me reading about the subject of women's rights. Should you count me a lady, then I should not have your leave to read the treatises. If I were counted a lady by you, I might require your endorsement, but since I am not a lady by your standards, I require nothing of the sort. It is a quandary, for if I were a lady by your standards, I would likely care about your opinion, yet

I do not."

He sighed. "I do believe you are overthinking it."

Lizzy gasped. "I shan't agree, sir. You have insulted me by insisting I am not a lady. I should perhaps care about your good opinion, but since I know it is lost and shall never be regained—"

He smothered an oath as his dipped suddenly, pulling her into his arms so his mouth could settle over hers. When she gasped in shock, his tongue slipped inside like an invader trying to conquer foreign territory.

She put her palms against his chest, having every intention of shoving him from her person.

Instead, her fingers dug into the fine velvet, and she pulled him closer. Her mouth strained against his in a fevered kiss, and she could scarcely breathe.

He pulled back a moment later, staring at her with his warm dark eyes. She was used to seeing them frosted by disdain, so the marked contrast was enough to steal her breath anew. She stared at him in shock, silence lengthening between them.

He smiled slowly. "You are no doubt a fine lady, Miss Bennet, but you do not kiss like one."

She gasped, raising her hand to slap him. He intercepted it, holding it away from their bodies, which were still far too close for propriety. "You are injurious and most disagreeable, Darcy."

"And you are warm and pliant, and I wish to kiss you again." His head lowered to do just that.

Lizzy was the one who broke the kiss this time, though her thoughts swam in her head. She gasped, struggling to contain her thoughts as his mouth pressed light kisses over her cheek and down the column of her throat. "What are you doing to me, Mr. Darcy?"

"I am doing nothing. I cannot resist you, though ample reasons exist for me to find the fortitude to do so."

She let out a sound of anger as she wrenched from him. "Again, you insult me. How dare you kiss me like that and then continue your verbal war?"

He blinked. "We are not at war."

"We most certainly are, Darcy." She sniffed at him as she tried to move around him.

"If so, then let us consider this night an armistice."

She tossed her hair, which was freed from its pins to spill around her head in a dark cloud. "Pretty words, but they mean naught. I must leave, and we shall not discuss this again."

He stepped aside with a wave of

his hand in a dramatic fashion.

Lizzy strode past him but stopped. She had forgotten her candelabra. She planned to retrieve it, but he came up behind her and wrapped his arms around her waist. Lizzy stiffened at his familiarity and tried to pull away. When his head descended, she held her breath. His lips tickled her ear as he asked, "Do you really wish to depart, Lizzy?"

She gasped when he kissed her earlobe and used her nickname. "Release me at once, sir."

"You are free to leave at any time," he reminded her, but he did not release her. Instead, he put his mouth on her neck and nipped her. Lizzy stiffened with fear, but also surprise. His mouth felt good on her neck. She had never imagined herself to be the kind of person who could respond to a man under such scandalous circumstances, but she had to reevaluate her self-opinion as his mouth slid higher. He nibbled on her earlobe and caused her to moan.

Drawing forth a reserve of willpower she had not known she possessed, Lizzy turned in his arms. "Stop right now..." she trailed off when their gazes locked. His were dark with passion, and his arms tightened around her. Illogically, she felt no fear.

Instead, his passion seemed to feed her arousal.

She did not protest as his lips settled on hers to gently explore their plump contours. When his tongue slid inside her mouth, she groaned. Her hands came up, at first to push him away, but she plunged them into his thick hair. Her entire body began to tingle as he deepened the kiss, and liquid heat flooded her quim.

When he lifted his head, she protested, then blushed at her forwardness. What was she doing, making love with a virtual stranger? Sanity started to return, but before it could find more than a tenuous purchase, his hands were on her breasts, and he stroked them through the satin dressing gown.

Her nipples hardened in response to his palms as he massaged her. Lizzy arched her back and cried out as his left hand made its way to the ties holding it own to undo them before slowly pulling it down far enough to free her breasts, now wrapped in linen from her nightdress and nothing else.

She gasped at him taking such liberties even as she allowed them, and more. She did not protest when Darcy pulled the loose neck of her nightgown down far enough to bare her breasts. Never had they been bared to a man before, and she had to fight the urge to cover them.

He cupped one in his hand and tweaked the nipple. "Beautiful," he growled in a voice full of passion.

His deep, rough purr sent shivers through Lizzy's body. Part of her was aware that it was wrong to allow this man to touch her in such an intimate way. Another part of her rejoiced in the liberties he took. Apparently, there was a dark side to her passions she had never known of before.

When his mouth supplanted his smooth hand, Lizzy could not hold in a moan. His tongue flicked around the engorged peak before it darted away, only to return seconds later to increase her tension. Lizzy grew even wetter and arched her hips as his mouth continued to wreak havoc on her senses.

He stepped back marginally, but just enough to strip off the dressing gown and nightdress underneath. The dress fell in a puddle at her feet. She stood nearly naked before him, wearing only one petticoat with a discreet slit at the center of her femininity. He got to his knees to peel down the petticoat, pausing every few inches to kiss a newly exposed area of flesh.

Lizzy abandoned herself to the sensations he provoked and tore at his dressing gown with urgent hands. He chuckled and leaned back to strip off the nightcap and dressing gown in one smooth motion. He stood up after that, pausing to strip off the nightshirt to reveal his nudity beneath. She flushed at the sight, certain she should look away, but unable to do so.

Then she was in his arms again, with her soft breasts pressed against his lightly haired chest. His hands cupped her arse and massaged her cleft. His bare flesh in such a private area made her gasp, and he swallowed it by taking her mouth in another hard kiss, this one more intense than any previous one.

She ached for him to touch the very heat of her and wriggled impatiently. He kissed her again as he moved one hand from her arse to stroke the outer lips of her quim. One finger teased her clit, and Lizzy's body shuddered.

Her legs went limp, and he held her up as he brought her to the white sofa, where he pushed her down. He crouched on the floor in front of her and gazed at the center of her, occasionally rubbing his thumb over her swollen, but neglected, clit. "You have a most pleasing cunny, dear Lizzy."

Rather than be embarrassed, his words emboldened her. "Touch me." Lizzy did not recognize her own voice. It was rough with passion, and there was an urgency she could not remember ever having experienced.

"Your wish is my command." He cupped her with his hand, gently grinding the palm of his hand against her lips.

"Higher."

He laughed and slipped a finger inside her panties. His touch was light and expert, and her pulse quickened. Her hips thrust in time with his caresses, and soon her body shuddered with climax. Her quim continued to contract, and he slipped two fingers inside her.

"Are you ready for me?"

She hesitated. If she said yes, there was no backing out. She had already gone too far with a stranger, but if they completed their union, she might not respect herself ever again. She would certainly ruin all chances for a respectable match.

Considering she refused to marry for any reason but love, that did not seem like such a problem. Would anyone have to know?

What if she got pregnant?

Before she could think too rationally, he wiggled his fingers, and she nodded. She ached, deep inside, when he withdrew his fingers from her quim lips and rose to his feet. He felt around in the pocket of the discarding dressing gown he retrieved from the floor before producing a leather pouch. He removed it and unrolled a semitransparent tube.

She frowned, eyes widening as he started to smooth it over his shaft. "What is that, Mr. Darcy?"

"A condom made from animal membrane. It is a barrier to prevent pregnancy."

Fascinating. She arched her brow. "You carry such a device with you everywhere, sir?"

His cheeks flushed, and he looked away. "Not as a rule."

She looked down as he slid on the condom. His cock was thick and pulsed with each beat of his heart. The head was engorged and so large it caused her eyes to widen. He was not overly long, but she knew he would fill her completely. Curly brown hair nestled at the base of his cock and obscured his balls. Lizzy reclined as he knelt between her thighs.

He gave her one last questioning look, obviously needing to hear her consent. "Yes," she whispered. She tensed, hoping it would not hurt too badly.

He moved forward to lie on her and used one hand to guide his cock into her tight quim. He moved slowly, stretching her untried flesh. Each time she whimpered, he paused until she nodded for him to continue.

"I fear this last thrust shall hurt, but then it will feel wonderful soon enough." He advised her of that before leaning forward awkwardly to take her mouth in a deep kiss. As he did so, he surged to the hilt inside her.

She gasped at the pain, pressing against his chest. "I do not wish to continue."

"Lizzy, pray, hold still for but a moment. If the pain does not lessen, I shall withdraw and not bother you again." He spoke through gritted teeth, and he seemed to be barely in control.

"I…" She opened her mouth to refuse, but she trailed off as he shifted slightly, and the intolerable pain suddenly became uncomfortable pressure. "Perhaps I shall give you a moment," she said primly.

"Good girl." He shifted again, and the pain lessened still.

She barely noticed when he moved from shifting to thrusting, as her body adjusted. As she had suspected, he was a snug fit. If she hadn't been so wet, their union would not have worked. His tender ministrations were making the act almost pleasurable, and the more he moved, the more she liked it. He surged deeply inside her, and when she gasped this time, it was with pleasure, not pain. She could feel his heart beating through his cock, as they remained motionless for a moment, until she was accustomed to his breadth. Then he rocked his hips, and she matched the age-old rhythm he set.

He thrust into her as deeply as he could, using one hand to grasp her hip, while his other hand tangled in her hair. Sharp pain flashed through her head when he tugged, and her quim spasmed with the unique stimuli. Lizzy tightened her thighs around his waist and strove to take in all his cock. Once her quim had adjusted to his size, it seemed to thirst for more of him. She pressed her breasts against his chest, and she moaned when the changed position caused his cock to rub against her pearl.

Lizzy could feel herself building toward something. She did not know what; only that she must achieve it. Instinctively, she tightened her quim to bring it about sooner. She hovered at the edge as he continued to thrust into her, and she whimpered when she could not find release. She dug her nails into his back so deeply she heard him yelp. She ignored his verbal protests and clutched him against her. She ached for release only he could provide.

Their gazes locked, and she was temporarily transfixed by the naked need reflected in his eyes, rimmed by thick, dark lashes. Did his need mirror hers? The heady sensation of giving into the forbidden swept through her, and she could not have torn her gaze from his if she tried. The fluid way they reflected his emotions—passion, hunger, tenderness, and something less definable—fascinated her. A flush swept across his cheeks as she continued to stare into his eyes, and his gaze slid from hers.

He kissed her on the mouth, and their tongues dueled, as his hand moved between their thrusting bodies. He pressed in on her clit and rotated slowly, until she started to come. Lizzy's quim tightened around his suddenly bulging cock, and she was distracted from trying to catch his eyes again. He had grown so hard that it hurt. He lightly pinched her nub as he thrust into her deeper than ever.

She bit her lip to avoid screaming when an orgasm swept through her. It ravaged her body and caused her to shudder. Her quim squeezed around him several times, and she clamped her thighs around his waist tight enough to cause him to grunt. With a muted cry, he spilled his seed and flooded her quim with warm wetness, though the condom muted the sensation.

When the last wave of pleasure had faded, he did not immediately withdraw. Instead, he gathered her close to him, with her head on his chest. She could hear the rocketing beat of his heart as her ear was pressed against it. It slowly faded in crescendo, until it approached almost normal. He finally withdrew from her and turned from her to deal with the condom.

Doubts immediately assailed her. Lizzy chastised herself for giving in to desire with a man she did not know. She had thrown away her virginity in a moment of passionate indiscretion. What would her Papa think of her if he knew?

She had worked herself into quite a state when he turned back to her. "I have to go," she said as soon as he entered the room. "I must return to my room before someone discovers us out of bed and together."

He frowned. "Come upstairs with me."

"What?"

"I had it all set up to happen

upstairs. Instead, my desire overwhelmed me, and I took you on the couch. Please come upstairs with me."

How could she when she had tarnished her own perception of herself so much already? How could she compound her error by repeating it? As Lizzy asked herself those questions, she followed him up the stairs, with him holding tightly to her hand, as though he was determined she would stay. It seemed like her legs were independent of her brain, and even self-disgust could not break the thrall he held for her.

The carpet was soft under her bare feet, and Lizzy felt

discomfited by her nudity. "Why did we not take time to dress? Oh, what have you made of me, Mr. Darcy?" She must creep downstairs and retrieve her clothing on the library floor before staff found it. That it was borrowed from Miss Bingley provided only the thinnest shred of deflection or doubt about to whom it belonged. If it was discovered, she would be ruined.

"You have done the same to me, Lizzy. I shall retrieve our clothing in a short time." As he spoke, he opened the first door on the left, and she could see he had indeed prepared the room.

She looked around as she eased

inside. Noting the myriad candles in holders scattered around the room. The bed was tucked back invitingly. "What is all this?"

"I heard you stirring and hoped I might find a way to persuade you to feel the passion I feel for you. I hastily lit candles and rushed after you, finding you in the library. My own desire bested me, and I took you on the sofa. I apologize for not making it properly memorable for you, Miss Bennet."

She jerked at the sound of her last name on his lips. "I do believe we are past Miss Bennet by now…Fitzwilliam."

He grimaced. "I prefer Will

among my closest friends." He pulled her closer, lifting her hand to his lips to kiss. "I count you my closest *friend*, Lizzy."

"What do you want from me, Will?" His name sounded odd to her ears and felt strange on her lips, but a thrill shot through her at its illicit use.

"I would like to make you Mrs. Darcy. I know you have an ill opinion of me—"

She put her fingers to his lips. "I do not. Rather, I do, but much of my ill feelings toward you have been ameliorated by this night." She frowned. "You do know I have no wish to marry for money or any other reason except love, good sir?"

He smiled, his gaze tender. "I have heard exaggerated rumors of the lengths to which Mrs. Bennet will go to secure her daughters' futures, but I have also heard you described as the stubborn daughter, who shall refuse all who ask for her. I believe there was an incident with a cousin of yours a few years ago?"

She groaned. "Do not remind me of Mr. Collins. He visited for a fortnight last year and expected to take me home as his bride. Lucky for Jane, she had measles while he visited and got to remain mostly in quarantine, for he would have fallen for her beauty, and she would have done her duty."

He frowned. "Does Miss Bennet consider it her duty to marry?"

Lizzy softened her tone. "Not as such. She would have seen the advantage to having married the man inheriting Longbourn and likely done it, but she would have been unhappy. I have never seen her truly happy until meeting Mr. Bingley."

"I would say they could not court and love in the span of a month, but I would be a liar, for I have fallen in love with you in that short amount of time. I do love you, Lizzy. I should never wish to ruin you, and if I did not love you and have every hope of you accepting my proposal, I would not have anticipated our wedding night." He spoke with impassioned honesty as he held her hand to his chest.

Lizzy stared at him for a moment, almost overwhelmed. He loved her. Considering how they had sparred, that should leave her indifferent, or even gloating at his unrequited affections—but they were not unrequited. She loved him as well, though she could not pinpoint when it had happened. "Yes, Will, I shall be happy to accept your proposal, and I am certain I can persuade my father it is my fondest wish that he accept as well."

He bent his head to kiss her feverishly. "You have made me the happiest of men, my love."

She giggled as she snuggled closer. "I can feel how happy you are. Perhaps you would like to show me once more before I am forced to return to my room before dawn breaks?"

"I live to serve your every whim, dear Lizzy." His lips covered hers again in a soul-stirring kiss that sealed the covenant of their love long before the wedding ceremony that would no doubt soon take place.

DARCY IN MOONLIGHT

BLURB

In this short, erotic reimagining of PRIDE & PREJUDICE, what would happen if Lizzy had come across Mr. Darcy skinny-dipping in a stream in Rosings Park the night before the disastrous Hunsford proposal? Could seeing him in a different light—moonlight—soften Lizzy toward him, and he to her? Will they avoid acrimony and instead find physical and emotional release as they confess their love and explore their mutual desires?

It was too stifling in Hunsford. Lizzy could not decide if that was from the over insulation in the small rectory, or if it was the company. Mr. Collins, being a man full of hot air, seemed to make the area around him stuffier with each frivolous word that passed through his lips.

She slipped out for a long walk, not bothering to tell anyone. It wasn't entirely proper to be traipsing around after dark without a chaperone, but she was on the grounds of Rosings Park. She could not imagine a scenario that compromised her or brought her harm.

She walked for a time, her feet idly directing her toward a stream she recalled cutting across the property. That sounded refreshing, and it looked even more so when it came into sight a short time later.

She walked down the incline and paused near the bank, prepared to sit and dip her feet into the gently running water. A flicker of movement made her freeze, and she withdrew into a clump of bushes. Lizzy focused on where she'd seen the motion, and it soon came again. There was someone in the stream!

Her eyes widened, and she stifled a gasp when she recognized the man in the water. Darcy floated on his back in the water, which clearly revealed he wore nothing. She barely stifled a gasp, along with the urge to let her gaze wander to his erect member. She wasn't entirely successful in her attempts to look away.

The moonlight lent his body a silver glow, and her thighs quivered as she stared at him. When he turned over, his buttocks emerged slightly above the waterline; just enough to provide a tantalizing peek that caused a rush of liquid heat between her legs.

Her nipples hardened, and she shifted restlessly to ease the brush of fabric against the swollen buds. Lizzy couldn't tear her gaze from Darcy as he finished his swim and walked from the stream. The water sluiced down his body in asymmetrical lines that invited her eyes to follow.

When he was thigh-deep in the water, she saw his engorged cock. It fully confronted her, making it impossible to look away. The wide shaft culminated in a thick head. The closer he got to shore, the more visible his cock became. Imagining how he might use that, having only a rudimentary understanding of coupling, made her whimper, and she pressed her hand tighter against her mouth.

He lifted his head, looking right at the bushes where she hid. "You might as well come out, Miss Bennet."

Heat suffused her face, making her cheeks hot. She huddled closer to the ground out of instinct.

"Come on now. I shan't hurt you." His voice turned from coaxing to smoky. "Let me see you."

Reluctantly, Lizzy stood up, pushing aside the foliage to step into his line-of-sight. It was impossible to meet his gaze, and she lowered her head as he walked toward her, making no effort to cover himself. Why had he not reached for his shirt, if nothing else?

"Why were you spying on me?" There was a teasing note in Mr. Darcy's tone.

He stood just inches from her, so close that droplets of water splashed her arm when he ran a hand through his hair. She forced her chin up to look at him, though she didn't directly meet his gaze. "I was not spying, I assure you. I was merely taking a walk, since the rectory is so stifling. I did not intend to meet anyone."

Darcy grinned at her. "Yet you have met me." He seemed utterly relaxed in his nude state, which surprised her, because he was normally so stiff and formal. Right now, he was just stiff.

Her face heated at the thought, and she quickly moved her gaze when she realized she was staring at his crowning glory. "Yes." She cleared her throat. "I wanted to…I didn't mean to…"

"I know what you want, Lizzy." He moved closer, pressing his damp chest to hers. The white dress absorbed the moisture from his skin like a sponge. If not for her chemise and stays, the fabric would be translucent, showing her breasts.

She tried to pretend like he hadn't said anything. "I wished to clarify with you about your cousin's words. He told me just this afternoon that you have kept Jane and Mr. Bingley apart." She resisted the urge to look down again. Barely. "I did not seek you out, but now that we are here, I must ask. Did you steer Mr. Bingley away from Jane?"

Darcy took another step forward, swallowing the rest of the space between them. "Yes." He breathed the word against the top of her head, and the sensation made shivers run up her spine.

Lizzy stared straight ahead at the curve of his shoulder. Outrage prickled anew. "How dare you be so presumptuous, Mr. Darcy? My sister loves Mr. Bingley, and he seemed fond of her, if not more."

"I doubt that." He wrapped his arms around her. "Miss Bennet seems distant and aloof in his presence. How am I to believe she cares for him?"

"Society requires a certain amount of distance. What right have you to judge the sincerity of her affections?" It was increasingly difficult to focus on her questions and not the feelings his touch provoked.

"I observed no great passion on her part." His voice dipped on the word passion.

She shivered, daring to glance at him briefly. "I assure you, her affection is sincere. You have done them a great disservice."

He made a sound low in his throat. "Very well."

She blinked. "What does that mean?"

He bent his head, his lips almost close enough to brush hers. "It means I shall defer to your judgment, Lizzy, and correct the course by encouraging Mr. Bingley to return to Netherfield. I am certain their courtship will progress from there without aide."

She cleared her throat. "Er, um, yes. Thank you?" She wasn't entirely certain he deserved gratitude, since he had been the one to cause the separation, but that he was willing to reconsider engendered warmth in her chest. Just appreciation and nothing more, of course.

"I ask for you to do something for me, Lizzy."

Her eyes widened as she met his gaze, realizing he had impertinently used her nickname twice now. "What, Mr. Darcy?"

"Stay away from Wickham."

She frowned, not liking his attempt to dictate to her. "I beg your pardon? I can choose my own friends, sir." She poked him in the chest for emphasis.

He reached out, capturing her hand and folding it in his damp one. "I assure you that man is no one's friend, especially a woman of quality."

She scowled. "Mr. Wickham has been a perfect gentleman." True, he had abandoned his seeming affections for her to get engaged to an heiress, but she knew young men required means to live.

"He is no gentlemen." His dark eyes flashed for a moment. "He attempted to seduce my sister last year and nearly led her to ruin. Georgiana was just fifteen at the time."

She gasped, searching his gaze. She could not doubt the sincerity she saw there. "I had no idea."

He inclined his head. "I thought as such."

"But Wickham—"

He pressed a finger to her lips. "I do not wish to further discuss that rake. Surely, you do not really desire to do so either? Is there not something you would rather be doing?"

She moaned when he arched against her, pushing his hard cock into her stomach. A wave of desire washed over her, making it impossible to think of anything else. "Yes," she whispered, surrendering to her need for Darcy. She drew his finger into her mouth to suck on the digit.

Then she blinked. "I mean no. This is scandalous. I shall be ruined if anyone knows we were out here alone, and you in such a state of dishabille."

Darcy laughed. "I cannot even classify this as dishabille."

She scowled at him. "How can you be so calm about this situation, Mr. Darcy? Do you not realize how this could affect both our reputations? If you compromise me, people will expect you to offer marriage. When you fail to do so, it will cost you any remaining goodwill, at least among the people of Hertfordshire, and perhaps even here."

"That would be most devastating," he said with a twitch of his lips. "As it happens, the fear is ungrounded."

She shook her head. "We are likely not the only ones still awake." She shuddered at the thought of Mr. Collins catching her in such a position. He would be thrilled for certain to have selected Charlotte in her stead. He would also immediately reveal her impropriety first to Lady de Bourgh and second, her papa.

"I meant the fear that I would not ask for your hand is ungrounded."

She snorted, a most indelicate sound. "What nonsense, Mr. Darcy. You dislike me. I have lost your good opinion, never to regain it."

"That is wrong. As it stands, I had planned to wait until tomorrow to declare my intentions, but it seems unwise to wait." His hands wrapped around her upper arms. "Allow me to express my ardent love and true affection for you, Lizzy. I have tried to fight it, but there is no withstanding emotion of such force."

She blinked at him, at first certain he was pulling a joke at her expense. "Most amusing, Mr. Darcy." She tried to pull away, but his damp hands tightened. "Release me."

"Not until I have your answer. Will you be my wife, Lizzy?"

The more she stared at him, the more convinced she became he was being sincere. Either that, or he needed a padded cell at Bedlam. "Have you taken leave of your senses, Mr. Darcy?"

"Undoubtedly," he said with a droll laugh. "Yet I can summon no regret for doing so. I love you, Lizzy. Will you marry me?"

"I can scarcely believe you."

He cupped her buttocks in his hand, pulling her tightly against him. "I want you. I have wanted you since the moment I saw you, despite my protestations to the contrary. You are a most handsome woman, and I was a fool to behave with such arrogance."

He brushed his thumb over her mouth and then drew in a deeper breath between his clenched teeth when she nipped his finger. "I do not care about your familial connections or any other flaws. You are the woman for me."

His words were seductive, and she had little reason to doubt them. Darcy could be arrogant and prideful, but he had always been honest to a fault in their interactions. She still bore anger at the colonel's revelation that he had tried to scupper the relationship between Jane and Mr. Bingley, but he seemed contrite and ready to stop interfering.

Could he be right about Wickham? The man was so utterly charming, but wouldn't that kind of façade serve him well if he really was a blackguard? To think he had tried to seduce and force Mr. Darcy's young sister into marriage by compromising her made Lizzy feel sick.

He lowered his head while withdrawing his finger from her mouth. Lizzy tipped back her head in order to meet his mouth, giving in to the heady desire threatening to overwhelm her suddenly. Sparks flared between them when their lips met. It was her first kiss, and it exceeded anything she had expected.

She parted her mouth to allow his tongue inside while trembling under the onslaught of sensations assaulting her. Her head spun, and she was too hot. The light dress was too constricting, and it was all she could do not to tear it off, along with the underlayers beneath.

Darcy cupped her shoulders in his hands as his mouth explored hers. Lizzy met each thrust of his tongue with her own, as her body gyrated against him of its own accord. She wanted to feel him inside her, to test the length of his cock with her folds, to ride him and feel him come inside her. Where were those scandalous thoughts coming from, and why were they so appealing?

She grasped a handful of his hair to pull his head away. Lizzy drew in a long breath before nuzzling his neck. She enjoyed the way he twitched as she nibbled the column of his throat, pausing to suck a spot here and there. He groaned when she stroked her tongue across the sensitive area, before grazing the bend of his neck with her teeth.

"My sweet, that feels intoxicating." He stroked a hand down her back and across her bum, pausing to squeeze one of her cheeks. Meanwhile, his other hand delved into the bodice of the dress in search of a breast, somehow easing between the layers and under her chemise. Lizzy gasped against his neck when he thumbed her nipple, in turn making him shiver.

"I want to taste you," he said in almost a growl.

The moonlight highlighted the passion in his eyes, but she wasn't frightened. Instead, evidence of his extraordinary desire excited her. She wanted all of him, not just the gentlemanly persona he hid behind most of the time. "I want that too."

To hell with propriety. He planned to ask her father for permission to marry her. If they were compromised, he would offer for her hand. She had no reason to hold back—at least not one as compelling as the need to go forward and entrust herself to his passionate care.

Darcy busied himself with stripping the dress from her, along with the chemise, petticoat, and stays. As soon as he disposed of the garments, Darcy lowered his head to suck her breast. Lizzy closed her eyes, grasping his shoulders to keep her feet as he licked the nipple before sucking on her breast. His rhythmic tugging and licking transmitted straight to her quim, and she tightened her thighs in an attempt to control the sensations.

Her head spun as Darcy lifted and carried her closer to the streambank. He lowered her onto what had to be his jacket. She laid back, parting her arms and legs to allow him full access. He hovered over her for a long moment. The moonlight caught his eyes, making them shine with his naked hunger. Her need matched his, and she reached for him. "Come to me, Darcy."

He took the hand she extended and knelt between her thighs, once again capturing her lips in a long kiss. His mouth seared hers, fusing them together for what seemed like an eternity. Her mind whirled, and her thoughts split into colored fractals as she lost herself in his embrace, reveling in the sensations flowing through her.

His mouth drifted lower, leaving her lips despite her efforts to keep him with her. When he licked her neck, she tensed before relaxing. He licked and sucked the sensitive area before sweeping his tongue across her throat and down her breastbone.

She exclaimed with surprise when he buried his head between her breasts to inhale deeply. "Darcy." Lizzy ran her hands through his hair, not sure for what she was asking. No, that wasn't right. She wanted him to do everything with her and to her. She just didn't know what to ask him to show her first.

Darcy rolled to bring himself into position with the breast he hadn't yet tasted. Lizzy sighed when he sucked the globe into his mouth, lapping greedily at her nipple. His tongue was raspy against the rigid bud, and she shifted restlessly, tightening her grip on his hair, inadvertently drawing him away.

He braced his chin on the side of her breast. "Is something wrong?"

She shook her head, and then said, "Yes."

With a smile, he sat up a bit, supporting his chin with one hand, while the other flirted with her quim. His pinkie traced her slit, running ever so lightly against her nub. She bit her lip to keep from screaming with frustration when he continued to stroke her nonchalantly, seemingly without any intent to actually dip inside her quim to explore deeper.

"What is the problem, sweeting?"

What was the problem? Lizzy shook her head, not sure what she wanted to tell him. "Never mind." She was too uncertain to voice what she wanted, especially since she didn't know the terms. She just wanted to feel more of the amazing sensations his ministrations evoked.

He lifted his shoulder in a half-shrug and lowered his head again, this time below her breast, to trace his tongue across her stomach in a circuitous route that brought him ever closer to her quim.

"Yes, there…" She moaned.

He froze, his tongue just below her belly button. When he exhaled, a wash of hot air bathed her quim, increasing her arousal. After a moment, Darcy started licking and kissing her skin again, but gave no indication he was about to plunge his tongue inside her.

With a frown, Lizzy tugged on his hair, making him look up at her. "I want you to taste me."

"I am about to," he said in a sexy purr, and the rumble of his voice emerging from his throat pulsated through her sensitive flesh, making her thighs contract.

"Please. I need…"

He arched his brow. "You do not want me to lick your sweet little quim?"

Lizzy sighed impatiently. "I do. Of course I do. Why does it feel so maddening though?"

"Because your body wishes to come." He smiled. "And so you shall…soon."

Lizzy laid back again, releasing

her hold on Darcy's hair. She let her arms fall out to her sides. Her legs mimicked the motion, opening wider to receive her lover as Darcy settled into position. His breath warned of his approaching tongue, but she had no desire to rebuff him. She was impatient to feel the foreign sensation of a man's mouth on her intimate parts.

Darcy took her quim with thorough mastery. With no hesitation, and with a sense of confidence emanating from him in waves, he consumed her. His mouth was a buffer that shielded her vulnerable flesh, covering her quim from the outside world. His tongue was an invader, probing her cunny from clit to opening in strokes that varied from short to long, from deep to the lightest touch.

Lizzy arched against him, riding his face instinctively. His mouth was hot and wet, just like her quim, and she welcomed his tongue the same way she would soon welcome his cock. That thought was almost terrifying, especially to an unmarried, not-yet-officially engaged proper young woman, but it also filled her with gleeful anticipation.

As he flicked his tongue across her clit in feather-light strokes, she sobbed, his name flying from her mouth in a jumbled wave of sound. Moisture filled her quim, and her womb contracted as she came hard under his mouth. Darcy lapped up every drop of her arousal, prolonging the waves of pleasure that spread from the omphalos of her quim.

It was only when she laid in a boneless heap, temporarily incapable of moving, that Darcy finally lifted his head. He gave her a wicked grin. "You are as delicious as I expected, Miss Bennet."

She managed a weak smile. "Thank you, Mr. Darcy." Tears blurred her vision, and she blinked them away. The orgasm had been more than physical. It had touched her on a primitive level, and she had to regain control of her emotions before she burst into song or hurled herself into his arms, a sobbing mess.

"It was all my pleasure." He licked the side of his mouth to remove the last traces of her juices. "Completely mine."

Lizzy shook her head. "Not completely. You have not been pleased."

"How do you know?"

She fumbled, unable to see from her vantage point, but soon finding the proof. His cock was hard and heavy in her hand, and she pumped the length, rubbing her palm against the head. "This tells me so."

Darcy's breathing was ragged. "Do you like what you feel, Lizzy?"

"Very much." She almost purred her satisfaction, feeling wild and wanton. "I want it to be inside me." She shifted to bring her quim closer to his cock. "I want your cock inside me, Darcy. Take me. Now."

He grinned, clearly amused, but also unable to hide a trace of male pride. "Who am I to deny you what you wish, dearest?"

"Take me," she said again. Where this streak of authority came from, she could not say. It was as though Darcy's mouth had unleashed an entirely heretofore unknown side of her.

He lifted her thighs atop his, and she locked them around his back. Lizzy held her breath as he aligned their pelvises, bringing the head of his cock against her opening. She arched against his shaft, longing to have him deep inside her. "Make me yours, Fitzwilliam." Saying his name felt entirely too bold, but it was nothing when compared to the liberties she had already granted and wanted to take.

Darcy eased inside an inch, and then two. Lizzy sucked her breath through her teeth, unaccustomed to such an intrusion in her untried body. It was uncomfortable for a second, but she endured.

"Relax, and the pain will fade, Lizzy." He was clearly gritting his teeth and appeared to be maintaining fierce control.

She did as he suggested, trying to relax as he slowly rocked into her, going deeper with each thrust. When he was buried to the hilt, she let out a small cry from the sharp sting, but it soon faded. He continued his slow thrusts, which started to feel more teasing than painful. "Take me completely, Darcy."

"You are a demanding chit." He sounded amused. A second later,

Darcy surged deeply inside her.

Lizzy closed her eyes, gritting her teeth to keep in a scream from the intense sensation of having him stretch and fill her so completely. He sank to the hilt, and she held him against her, locking her legs tighter still, in an effort to keep him from moving. There was another moment of pain as her virginity was absolutely destroyed, but pure bliss to be joined with him soon followed.

Soon, Darcy shifted against her. She uttered a sound of protest as he withdrew, but it turned to an exhalation of pleasure when he plunged into her again, once more filling her. She surrendered to the pace he set, letting his rhythm determine hers as they engaged in a primal dance as old as time. Their simpatico thrusts had them both grunting and moaning, and she saw the veins bulging in his forehead as he increased his force.

"Harder. Deeper," she demanded, wanting to sink completely into Darcy, until they were one being. He complied, and she cried out with pleasure. Convulsions built inside, spreading outward, and when her sheath contracted around his cock, Darcy groaned, releasing spurts of satisfaction inside her.

His hot fluid filled her, and she

tightened her legs into a vise to hold him for a long second. They stayed without moving as he emptied his passion into her, while she convulsed around him. Her heartbeat thundered in her ears, and all she could hear was their harsh breathing as she loosened her legs, letting Darcy withdraw.

He rolled onto his side, bringing her with him. His arm held her against him, and his uneven breath blew over her neck. Lizzy literally couldn't move because she was so sated. "I did not know it would be like that," she finally managed to say.

"Neither did I." He pressed a

kiss to her cheek.

"You were a virgin too, Mr. Darcy?"

He shifted and sounded a little discomfited when he answered. "No, but the few encounters I have experienced were nothing like this. I believe love is the difference, Lizzy."

A wave of anxiety washed over her then. "You will come to Hunsford tomorrow?"

"Yes, dearest, and then on to Longbourn to be assured I have your father's blessing and permission to marry you."

She sighed, finding no reason to doubt him. "It is most peculiar that I was convinced you were a disagreeable, prideful man, for whom I had no regard, until this very night, Mr. Darcy."

He chuckled. "Perhaps you saw my assets in a new light, Lizzy."

"Perhaps it was the moonlight."

FIRST NIGHT AS MRS. DARCY

BLURB

In this short erotic variation of PRIDE & PREJUDICE, it is the wedding night of the ardent couple. Lizzy has doubts and fears, but Fitzwilliam will guide her through each one until she discovers her own wanton nature as they please each other and become truly married as only consummation can ensure.

Lizzy had never been in Fitzwilliam's bedchambers before, of course, but she spent a moment admiring the elegant surroundings. Or she gave the appearance of doing so, but in fact, she barely noticed the luxurious furnishings, dark cherry wood, and silver and navy color scheme. Instead, her attention shifted and remained glued to Fitzwilliam.

As soon as the door had clicked shut behind them, he unbuttoned his jacket and dropped it carelessly across the wingback chair nearest the door. Her mouth watered with anticipation as she waited for him to finish undressing.

Anticipation and a strong dash of anxiety. Would it hurt terribly? Would she enjoy her wedding night? Would Mr. Darcy—Fitzwilliam—find her pleasing? Those fears plagued her as she stood in her dress, watching as her new husband slowly tugged at his cravat.

Apparently, Fitzwilliam wasn't in a rush, because he contented himself with removing the cravat and unbuttoning his waistcoat, but he stripped no further. Her stomach dipped with disappointment, even though the idea of just jumping into nakedness was a bit daunting.

He sat down on the sofa, patting the cushion beside him. "Come join me, Lizzy."

She laid her reticule on the chair he'd chosen as a coat rack before walking over to join him. Licking dry lips, she sat on the cushion beside him, wondering what was in store for her. Her mother had given her unclear and unhelpful instructions on what to expect. Hill had tried to tell her more, but the serving woman had blushed and backed away before she could finish describing what a wedding night entailed.

In her quest for knowledge, she had considered writing to Lydia to ask her about the mysteries of a wedding night, but she had reconsidered. The idea of the letter being seen by George Wickham was too shameful to bear. She could not bear the humiliation if he knew she was asking her youngest sister about sex.

Just thinking the word was enough to make her shiver, though she couldn't decide if it was from excitement or fear. Perhaps both. Perhaps it was knowing she was about to explore the enigma of Fitzwilliam Darcy that had her nerve endings thrumming and her palms sweating. She blotted them discreetly on her dress.

Fitzwilliam's mouth lifted in a half-grin as he pulled her back against the couch, while angling her closer to him. "I must say, I feel somewhat like a virgin."

Lizzy looked at him solemnly. "Are you not a virgin, Mr. Darcy?"

"As my wife, you are permitted to use my first name." His lips brushed her cheek when he teased her. "Dear Lizzy, I have known women before, but none that I have loved or admired in such high esteem as you. I want the evening to be perfect for you."

"I wish it to be perfect for you as well, dear husband."

Fitzwilliam chuckled softly. "I

have no doubt it shall be a night to remember, my love."

"I confess I do not know what to do." She pleated a handful of her lovely wedding dress, sewn just for the double wedding. It made her feel slightly better to know Jane was going through a similar experience with Charles at this very moment.

"It is a simple matter on the surface, but there are many ways to please each other." He took her hand in his and brought it to his mouth to kiss the back. "There is kissing, of course."

She flushed, recalling the bold kiss he'd claimed from her just days ago in the parlor, when they'd had the space to themselves for a few short moments. Just thinking of it made her squirm.

He eyed her for a moment. "Tell me your thoughts."

"I was recalling our kiss. It makes me feel breathless and tingly just to think about it." She couldn't bring herself to specify where she tingled.

Fitzwilliam must have read her mind, or he had a vast store of knowledge. "Does it tingle between your legs?"

She flushed and looked away. "Yes, sir."

His fingers were gentle on her chin when he turned her back to face him. "Do you feel wet there as well, Lizzy?"

She looked down, too shamed to answer.

"Come now, love. If you do not answer, I shall have to find out for myself."

She looked up, eyes wide with alarm. "Are you allowed to do so?"

Fitzwilliam chuckled. "We are married now. There is nothing we aren't allowed to do with each other as long as we both desire it. Should I touch your quim, Lizzy?"

She blinked. "What is a quim?"

"The spot between your legs. It is also called a cunny. I promise you will most fervently enjoy the touch." He brushed his lips against her mouth in a light kiss.

"But it is too soon for that."

He moved closer, lowering his head. His mouth was inches from hers. "You have the most beautiful lips." He exhaled raggedly. "Utter perfection."

"What is?" Lizzy found it difficult to drag in a deep breath as his mouth edged closer to hers. Waiting for his mouth to settle on hers was killing her. She curled her hands into fists against her legs.

"You." Finally, Fitzwilliam bridged the distance still separating them. His lips teased hers with a gentle stroke as he tentatively tasted her.

Lizzy twined a hand in his thick

locks, bringing him closer to deepen the kiss. His mouth curved to hers as though made by design. Heat sparked where their lips fused, spreading through her like a wildfire. She parted her lips to welcome his probing tongue. It swept into her mouth, searching the depths while eliciting shivers that raced up her spine. Lost in the moment, she had no concept of time or space. The kiss was more intense than the previous one, and it burned her to the core.

Her nipples pressed against the silky lining of her chemise, in turn aggravated by the friction with the material when she shifted to move closer to Fitzwilliam. Lizzy gasped when Fitzwilliam grasped her hips to lift her onto his lap. Her thighs straddled his, and her breasts pressed against his chest. It relieved the abrasion from the lining, while the pressure from his body added a new level of sensitivity, heightening her arousal.

Fitzwilliam broke the kiss to slide his mouth down her chin, across her throat, and to the bend at her neck. "Forgive me for rushing you, Lizzy, but I cannot bear to have distance between us." He caught the delicate flesh between his teeth, nipping her gently.

She moaned, arching her back.

He placed a hand between her shoulder blades, holding her taut against him. "You taste like fresh peaches and cream," he said against her ear. His tongue traced her lobe, making her squirm. "You are most addictive, love." He drew the lobe between his teeth to graze her. Lizzy clutched his dark hair with one hand, anchoring herself with the other around his neck. "I long to taste every inch of you."

He breathed into her ear, making her cry out even as she nearly fainted from the shocking image that came to her as she imagined Fitzwilliam tasting every spot on her body. He could not mean every single one, of course.

The thought made her tremble, and every nerve in her body sang with arousal, stirring her to a fever pitch. "Yes, please," she said, encouraging Fitzwilliam when he unbuttoned her dress slowly. The bodice drooped and fell open to reveal her stays and the chemise underneath. With impatient movements, he undid the hooks of her stays and tossed the corset over his shoulder without regard for where it landed.

The dress pooled at her waist, and only her chemise preserved her modesty. Lizzy reached up to cover her nipples, which were poking through the thin material of the chemise.

"Do not cover yourself." As Fitzwilliam issued the command, he lifted her to her feet. He moved with precision and the same sort of skill as their maid at home as he stripped off the outer dress and her petticoats beneath.

Finally, he bent partially to grasp the hem and pull the chemise up and over her head. She lifted her arms to assist with the removal. That left her breasts brazenly bared, and she could scarcely stand to look at her husband in her mortification. "Please extinguish the candles, Fitzwilliam."

"Never. You are absolutely

perfect, and I desire to see all of you," said Fitzwilliam, sounding awed. He cupped her breasts in his palms, squeezing lightly. "Your breasts are those of a true gentlewoman, Lizzy. They are the perfect amount, the perfect texture, and the most perfect pink nipples." He thumbed them as he spoke, teasing them so that they tightened almost painfully.

"I cannot tell about your state of perfection." She chided him for remaining mostly dressed, though it was embarrassing to do so. Her voice was husky with passion, sounding unlike her. She framed his face with her hands, pausing for a long kiss before speaking again. "I suspect you are a perfect specimen without your garments, husband."

Fitzwilliam laughed softly. "I suppose you wish me to disrobe?"

Lizzy kissed him again, nodding as she worked her mouth on his, her lips tracing his. She sucked in his lower lip to nibble on it, and Fitzwilliam's body jerked beneath her. "Perfect," she said against his lips. How did she become so bold? Surrendering to her instincts seemed to be guiding her in the proper direction, so she endeavored to relax and try to fret less about her fears.

Fitzwilliam was finally all hers. She should enjoy every moment of that.

Fitzwilliam lifted her higher, breaking contact with her mouth, to bring her breasts closer. She closed her eyes, letting her head fall back when he lowered his head to taste one of her breasts.

Exhaling through her teeth kept her from shouting her pleasure when he licked the contour of her breast, slowly swirling his tongue around the areola before homing in on her nipple. When he sucked the bud into his mouth, she couldn't stifle a whimper. Nor could she keep her hips from bucking against his stomach. Liquid heat pooled in her quim, and her nubbin pulsed with need as he sucked.

Fitzwilliam tested the contours of her breast with maddening thoroughness. His tongue swirled over every inch before his lips repeated the process prior to returning to her nipple. She moaned, once again thrusting against him in search of relief. He raked his teeth across the sensitive bud, and she grasped handfuls of his hair, not sure if she wanted to end the discomfort by pushing him away, or if she wanted to pull him closer, to encourage him to bite harder.

He made the decision for her by slowly, carefully applying more pressure with his teeth. A prick of pain accompanied the action, but it faded when he soothed the nipple with his tongue. The swipe of his tongue over the peak made her cry out. In an attempt to ease the ache in her quim, she tightened her thighs around his hips and lifted herself higher to push her quim more firmly against his tight stomach.

He still wore too many layers between them, and she pulled from his grasp, lowering her feet to the floor instead of having him holding her in a standing position.

Fitzwilliam cupped her hips. "What troubles you, my love?"

"I want you to be bare to me, Fitzwilliam." Lizzy licked her lips, still tasting his essence on them. "I want you nude so I may touch every inch of you." Her cheeks bloomed with color as she made the confession. She quickly sat down in a nearby wingback and distracted herself by removing her garters and stockings.

He chuckled. "I endeavor to please you." As he spoke, Fitzwilliam finished undoing the last button of the waistcoat and removing it. His breeches were next, and she looked with inquisitiveness at the fall as it opened. She could not see enough of him to satisfy her curiosity.

He removed his pants and stood before her in only his shirt for a long moment. Then he stripped it off, and her husband was revealed. She stared at him with appreciation, though the size of his erection was a little daunting. She had a vague idea that it must enter her body somewhere. Her quim was the most likely spot, but she doubted she could accommodate him.

Fitzwilliam leaned back against the sofa, palms splayed on the cushions. He didn't move, making it clear that she should take the initiative. While she could easily envision climbing atop him again and sliding her body against his, it took her a moment to stride forward.

She was too taken by the mouthwatering sight of his erect cock jutting upward, as if challenging her to look away. Long and thick, it curved slightly, angling the purple head in such a way that she could see it perfectly. A drop of liquid quivered on the tip before rolling down his cock.

She yearned to intercept the droplet before it disappeared into his curly dark pubic hair, but it was gone even as the thought crystallized. She had never had such a thought before, and she marveled at the boldness of her thoughts.

Finally, Lizzy stepped toward him, standing before him.

"Please get on your knees, Lizzy. I shall show you the first way to please me before reciprocating."

With a small frown, she did as he instructed, staring up at him expectantly. "What shall I do know, Fitzwilliam?"

"Kiss my prick, Lizzy."

Her eyes widened, and the idea was shocking. "I cannot."

"You can. It will please me. If you are of the passionate nature I suspect, it might even please you."

She was still doubtful as she bent forward. Fitzwilliam's sharp inhalation and the spasm of his stomach muscles betrayed his reaction. She gave him a prim kiss on the tip of his cock. "Now what, sir?"

He laughed, though he sounded strained. "I was perhaps not explicit enough with instruction. Take the shaft into your mouth, dear Lizzy. Stroke me with your tongue and apply friction with your cheeks."

She remained doubtful of the feasibility but did as he instructed. His sharp groan made her freeze as she took the shaft into her mouth, but his gentle hand in her hair encouraged her to keep going.

She cupped his prick in one hand as her mouth neared the head. Lizzy shifted slightly, to be more comfortable and have better reach, and then licked the tip of his cock. Fitzwilliam jerked in her hand, and she pumped her palm up and down the length slowly, alternating between squeezing tightly and holding him loosely.

"Just like that, love," he said as she lowered her head.

Lizzy glanced up, pleased to see he'd thrown back his head. His eyes were closed, and the tendons in his neck had distended under the pressure of how tightly he'd clenched his teeth. In a second, she took his cock deeper into her mouth.

It was difficult to accept all of him, and she struggled to relax her jaw and take him in. When she had truly relaxed, his member slid freely between her lips. Fitzwilliam pumped his hips in response, feeding more of his cock to Lizzy. It took her a moment to adjust to the length, but relaxing her throat helped her accept all of him.

"Move your head, dear wife."

Doing as he asked, she bobbed her head and cradled his balls in her palm, stroking him gently. She tightened her palm around the base of his cock and pumped him to the rhythm she set with her head. She didn't know if she had good form, but Fitzwilliam seemed to enjoy her ministrations.

Fitzwilliam groaned and arched as she sucked him, making Lizzy want to send him over the edge. She didn't know fully what to expect but inferred there was something coming. This act must surely culminate in an intense wave of pleasure.

She might not know proper technique, but she knew this was about pleasing him, but also about asserting herself and establishing that she had the power to make him come undone. The idea of having authority over any aspect of a man as strong and virile as Fitzwilliam thrilled her in a primal way, making her folds slicker than ever.

The convulsions from his shaft pulsed against her palm, letting her know something was changing. Lizzy waited until his stomach was tight, and his cock was stiffer than it had been. He tangled a hand in her hair as he let loose with a shout of satisfaction.

Her mouth was overrun with his fluid in that moment. She choked and gasped in shock as it continued to pour into her in spurts. She might have pulled away, but his hand tightened. He clearly wanted her to swallow what he was producing.

Lizzy drank in his completion with difficulty. Even after he had stopped trembling and had gone semi-rigid, she held him between her lips for a few seconds longer.

Eventually, Lizzy had to break the connection, and she met his gaze as she stood up to straddle his thighs.

Satisfaction warmed his eyes, and his lazy half-smile spoke of how much she had pleased him. "Thank you."

"You are welcome." It was such a formal response that was at odds with the intimacy of the act but seemed appropriate.

"I apologize for not warning you I was about to come, Lizzy. I got carried away with the pleasure of your mouth and forgot your inexperience." He stroked her arm as he spoke.

She nodded. "It was strange but

not unpleasant." Her cheeks flushed as she remembered her thoughts about holding power over her husband. She couldn't deny she had very much enjoyed that aspect indeed.

"Now it is my turn." Fitzwilliam wrapped his hand around her waist, lifting her higher.

"Um hmm." Lizzy arched her hips, rubbing her quim against his skin as he slowly dragged her up his body. The subtle changes in texture stimulated her in different ways, having her thrusting against his stomach, and then clenching her muscles when his chest hair tickled her sensitive lips.

After what seemed like an eternity, Fitzwilliam finally had her where he wanted her. He had slid down while sliding her upward, and she was now kneeling on the sofa, knees on either side of his head. She held her breath when he penetrated her folds with his thumb, working the digit deeply inside her. It was beyond her limits of self-control to resist thrusting against his hand. She cried out with relief when a second finger joined his thumb to fill her more completely.

"You have a beautiful quim, Lizzy." His breath washed over her pubic hair, tickling and making her surge toward him, wanting to feel his mouth inside her. "So tight." He wiggled the fingers inside her, as though stretching her. "I cannot wait to feel this sweet little quim riding me."

She mumbled something unintelligible, trying to give her consent to bypass oral pleasure and just take her. Every nerve in her body sang, crying out for his cock.

"First…" He licked her slit. "Just a taste."

No, perhaps she was not ready to skip this exquisite pleasure just yet. "More."

Fitzwilliam chuckled, and her

clit spasmed at the rush of warm air it produced. "Of course, my love. I shall never tire of licking your cunny." He licked her again, this time plunging his tongue inside her folds to swirl around her clit a couple of times.

When his mouth withdrew again, she could have cried with frustration. "Blast, Fitzwilliam, will you—"

When he engulfed her quim with his mouth, she broke off in mid-sentence, no longer capable of speaking as he sucked and licked her quim. The heat of his invading tongue made her hotter than she'd been, and she bucked her hips, pushing down against his mouth as he sucked her nub. His fingers continued to pump into her, while he worked her clit and the surrounding area.

Being at his mercy was just as pleasurable as having him at hers, she decided. That was her last truly coherent thought as Fitzwilliam alternated sucking, licking, and nibbling her cunny. She rocked her hips, thrusting against his face. Tremors radiated from her womb, and she tightened her thighs in preparation of the approaching orgasm.

Lizzy clenched her hands into the cushions of the couch, sobbing Fitzwilliam's name as he sucked her clit forcefully, and then blew against the little nub. Waves of satisfaction crashed over her, sweeping her into the onslaught. She had never known anything like it and nearly screamed from the intensity.

Convulsions racked her body, and she was only vaguely aware of Fitzwilliam slipping out from underneath her. She settled lower on the couch, still on her knees, and rested her forehead against the back of the sofa as her heart raced.

Before she barely had a chance to recover, he sat beside her. Lizzy wondered if she had the energy to move to his lap. Maybe he sensed how thoroughly the climax had ravaged her, because he lifted her around the waist and settled her on his lap.

"There is a bed," she managed to whisper in a husky voice.

"Later." He dismissed the idea by aligning their bodies. Lizzy's eyes widened when the head of his erection settled into her slick folds. "This might hurt, my love."

She gritted her teeth and nodded. Having his fingers surge inside her had been uncomfortable at times, so she could only imagine how much harder it would be to accept his full length. "I am ready."

He rocked gently against her

opening as his fingers started strumming her nubbin. She thrust against him on instinct, and his cockhead breached her channel. She gasped at the intrusion, but it wasn't painful. It was just unfamiliar.

He increased the intensity of his stroking, coaxing her to rock against him and take more of his cock with each thrust. Within minutes, he breached her tight channel, pushing past the barrier of her innocence, and making her whimper at the pain.

"Stay the course, my love. It will feel better soon." Fitzwilliam's forehead was beaded with perspiration. This was clearly costing him effort as well.

With the next mutual thrust, he was fully inside her. She cried out at the intrusion. "I wish to stop now, husband."

"Give it a bit more time, Lizzy." His tone was soothing, and his fingers were busy making her feel good.

It was almost enough to mask the pain from his possession. She closed her eyes and tried to compartmentalize the pain. As he withdrew and thrust again, it was less painful. Soon, his fingers were coaxing her toward another orgasm and making the dull pressure/pain in her cunny less noticeable. When it stopped hurting, she relaxed against him.

Fitzwilliam set a slow pace after that, thrusting deeply into her before withdrawing almost completely, and then repeating the motions. Lizzy circled her hips to rub her clit against his shaft as he filled her. Time seemed to lose any meaning as she rode him, their gazes locked. She took his hands, and they thrust in synch. The moment was more than sexual, and the intimacy she was sharing with Fitzwilliam was perfect.

It was almost an afterthought when they came again. Lizzy clenched around his cock as she climaxed, triggering his release deep inside her. That was an interesting sensation, and it enhanced the contractions still pulsing her sheath.

They continued to thrust against each other, their pace gradually slowing until they weren't moving at all. They remained joined, silence surrounding them. It was comfortable, and she felt no need to speak. Instead, she laid her head on her husband's shoulder and savored the silence of their perfect union.

LIZZY'S DESIRES

BLURB

In this short, reimagined version of PRIDE & PREJUDICE, Darcy is Lizzy's guardian. She was prepared to accept Wickham's proposal, but when Wickham changes his mind, it gives her a chance to truly express her forbidden desires to Fitzwilliam. Will the honorable man be able to withstand Lizzy's desires?

George Wickham was a rake and a scoundrel. "I cannot believe he refused the marriage contract, Fitzwilliam." She looked up sadly at her guardian, the man who had looked after her and her sisters for the past few years after their parents both died from cholera. The man she was secretly in love with and wanted to marry far more than she ever had Wickham.

"I hated to be the one to bear the sad news." He didn't sound all that sad about it. Fitzwilliam's arm around her tightened while the other rubbed her back. "He wanted too large a dowry."

She sniffled. "I am not worth

that?"

He smoothed a hair back from her face. "Oh, dear, it is not that. I feared he would fritter it away and leave you penniless."

"Oh." She sniffed again. "He said he loved me. He told me we should anticipate our wedding night. Once he signed, we were going to…" Lizzy trailed off, embarrassed to admit to her guardian what she'd planned to do with her suitor before learning he wanted money more than her. She was twenty, still a virgin, and was likely to die a spinster. Why couldn't she be lucky like Jane, who had snapped up the utterly suitable Mr. Bingley?

"Your first time should be special." Fitzwilliam's tone was gruff, in an odd way. "It should most certainly be after your wedding night."

Lizzy nodded, though she was not convinced a wedding was necessary to share passion. "I wish he were more like you, Fitzwilliam." She blinked back tears as she turned her head to look up at her guardian. "More caring and sweet. More handsome. Sexy…" She didn't know what compulsion seized her, but suddenly, she stretched her head and kissed her guardian on the lips. Not a tender peck of affection, but a slow kiss full of tender passion.

He jerked away, his gaze conflicted. "Lizzy?"

She bit her lip. "Oh, Fitzwilliam, I love you. I have always loved you, but not in the way I should." Lizzy bent her head, too embarrassed by her confession to meet his gaze. "Wickham appeared to be a suitable match, but my heart never belonged to him. I want someone else to take my virginity." She looked up again. "I want you, Fitzwilliam. Will you make my first time special?"

He seemed torn. "That isn't right, my sweet. We are not married, and I am older..."

She nodded. "I know. I am wrong to feel this way about you. There must be something wrong with me."

He shook his head. "No, and I refuse to have you think that. Of course, I have thought about you like that. I am still a man, and you are a beautiful woman. That you are my ward does not make your figure less attractive or your sweet breasts less tempting. It does not keep me from thinking about your tight quim while stroking myself at night."

"Fitzwilliam?" she asked with tentative hope.

His shoulders sagged when he let out a long sigh. "I shall show you just how special your first time should be, Lizzy." Fitzwilliam lowered his head, brushing his lips against hers in the lightest of kisses. "If you are sure this is what you want?"

Lizzy craved another one of those kisses, but deeper and longer. Her hands itched to touch him, and she couldn't resist conjuring mental pictures of the two of them tangled on his massive bed. "I am sure, Fitzwilliam," she whispered, still feeling timid.

"Very well then." Finally, he guided her head closer, holding her tautly against him as his mouth settled over hers.

Fitzwilliam kissed her thoroughly, his tongue pushing between the seam of her lips to explore the interior.

Lizzy did her best to mimic his motions before sensations overwhelmed her, and she couldn't consciously think about doing anything. Instead, she was guided by impulse and pushed her quim against Fitzwilliam's cock, rubbing her wet cunny against his hard flesh through the myriad layers of their fabrics. His breeches provided delicious friction but seemed like an unbearable barrier to what her young body sought out instinctively.

Fitzwilliam trailed his mouth

from her lips and across her cheek, to her ear. As he nibbled and sucked on the lobe, she arched her neck, continuing to rub against him in a way that seemed to aggravate the ache inside her. "Oh, Fitzwilliam, I need…" She broke off, not entirely sure what she needed.

He lifted his head. "Sweetness, I know what you need." He stood up abruptly, and she locked her legs around his waist as he carried her across the hall to his bedroom and placed her on his bed. Fitzwilliam shed his jacket, cravat, waistcoat, shirt, and breeches as he stood over her where she laid on the bed.

His body was hard and firm in all the right places. For a man who was just shy of thirty-five, he didn't look it. Her eyes widened at the sight of his cock. It was daunting. She had never seen one in person, of course, but Jane had coyly alluded to what she could expect on her wedding night.

That it wasn't her wedding night didn't bother her. That Fitzwilliam wasn't her husband did. Not because of social norms, but because she loved him and wanted to be with him forever.

After getting naked, he turned his attention to stripping her of the attire she'd picked so carefully. His long fingers were nimble with the buckles of the shoes. Even such a simple task as removing the flats was rendered sensual by his slow strokes and gentle exploration. Lizzy gasped with surprise when he brought one of her feet to his mouth, sucking on the big toe in a way that dragged at the pit of her stomach and made her squeeze her thighs.

Fitzwilliam released her toe. "You taste delicious. I shall enjoy a more leisurely exploration next time."

She thrilled at his confident assurance there would be a next time and nodded. "Are you sure? You might need to taste more to be certain, Fitzwilliam." It was liberating, but a bit scary, to be teasing Fitzwilliam in a sexual way. The whole experience was a mixture of both.

His eyes sparkled. "That can be arranged." Taking a step back, he examined her for a moment before urging her up in strategic ways to remove the long dress. He laid it carefully aside before returning to her. In the interim, she shimmied out of her petticoats and stays. She was removing her chemise when he returned to her. Aware of his gaze on her, she slowed down her movements to pull the white linen slowly over her head, until she was naked.

As his gaze rested on her breasts,

her nipples tightened, but she suddenly clapped her hands over them. He frowned and reached for her hands. Lizzy resisted his attempts to pull them away. "I am too small," she whispered.

Fitzwilliam shook his head. "Your breasts are perfect."

At his words, she stopped trying to cover them and let him move her hands. He got onto the bed with her, straddling her thighs as he leaned forward. Fitzwilliam pinned her wrists above her head, pushing her arms into the mattress as he lowered his head.

He kissed her for a long moment before moving his mouth to the side. Pausing near her ear, he said, "I think your breasts are gorgeous as they are, with those pointy little pink nipples. A perfect mouthful." Fitzwilliam trailed his tongue across her chest and over her left breast, pausing to swipe the nipple.

"Oh." His words were deliciously naughty "Do you like that?" she whispered.

"Mmm, I love this." He took more of her nipple into his mouth, his hands still holding hers against the bed. "It is plump and delicious," he added after sucking for another minute.

She was breathless. "Thank you, Fitzwilliam."

Fitzwilliam let go of her hands

to cup her breasts, pushing them together so the nipples almost touched. She gasped when he ran his tongue back and forth across both rapidly, occasionally flicking with the tip of his tongue or pausing to suck one. The sensation was indescribable, and her quim was soaking wet in no time. She writhed under him, arching her hips, and lifting her buttocks off the bed as she sought relief. "Fitzwilliam, please, I cannot…"

He laughed but lifted his head. "You can, sweetness."

Lizzy shook her head. "I shall die if you keep doing that."

Grasping her hips, he shifted his

weight and moved her higher up the bed. He nudged her thighs apart, settling between them to put his face against her slit. He inhaled deeply before exhaling against her. His breath teased the sensitive flesh, and she whimpered, lifting her butt higher.

"Sweet," he said, sounding pleased and surprised. He licked one of her outer lips, trailing his tongue down the length, to her taint, and then back up the other lip, seeming to take extra care not to touch her clit. "I should not be tasting you, but I cannot regret it. I must have you now, Lizzy, and I shall keep you."

"Yes." Her heart pounded. It sounded like Fitzwilliam intended to be her lover, not just a one-time event. Or was she misreading things? Was she trying to project more intent than was there? Would he keep her as his mistress now that she was allowing him to ruin her? It was a fearful prospect, but she couldn't bring herself to stop what was happening.

Fitzwilliam ran the broad part of his tongue across her slit, the appendage squirming in to explore her. He swirled the tip around her clit a few times as she bucked mindlessly under him, before continuing his swipe downward, to dart his tongue in and out of her opening several times.

Then he did something so shocking that she grabbed a handful of his hair and screamed his name. His tongue went lower, sweeping down her taint toward the dark hole waiting there. She cried out in protest when he breached the puckered ring. "Stop, Fitzwilliam. You cannot."

He paused, looking up briefly. "You do not like it?"

"Uh…I do not know." She hadn't really had a chance to experience the sensations. The act had just been too outrageous, and she had reacted.

"In that case…" Fitzwilliam

trailed off, returning to the forbidden zone. His tongue teased and tickled her asshole, briefly darting inside and around the hole. A feeling like electricity sparked through her lower half, and she pressed her ass tighter against his face.

Fitzwilliam chuckled against her skin. "Thought so," he said with triumph, before returning to his taboo task. A moment later, he slipped a hand between her thighs, his finger and thumb seeking out her clit. He rolled the sensitive bud between his fingers as his tongue flicked over and into her back passage.

Lizzy twisted against him, her

lower half completely off the bed, except for her heels. "Fitzwilliam. Oh, it is so much. Too much." Slick heat drenched her seconds before her cunny tightened, and an orgasm rushed over her, making her entire body shake with the force of it.

"Good girl," he praised, as though she had done something amazing, when it was all him. She had just been at his mercy. Apparently, she was still at his mercy, because he shifted again, once more putting his mouth against her cunny, with his hands gripping her buttocks. He pulled her tightly against him, not allowing her room to squirm or escape as he began licking her quim in earnest.

Powerless, Lizzy held onto the bedcovers with both hands, hating the way his hold constrained her movements, even as she recognized how much it heightened her pleasure. There was literally no escaping Fitzwilliam's hot, questing mouth. His only concession to her next release was a brief cessation of sucking and swirling, but then he wrung another and another climax from her, barely letting her finish the previous one before causing another.

After her last orgasm, she eyed his cock as she licked her lips. "I am not even sure that will fit in my mouth." It was a half-teasing, half-serious declaration.

He made his cock jump by flexing his muscles. "We should find out."

Lizzy smiled, finding it easier to move as the languid pleasure slowly faded from her body. "Yes, we should." She slithered down the bed a bit, turning on her side to face his cock. The head nudged against her lips, and she parted them to take a small taste of his pre-cum.

He was salty, but with an underlying hint of sweetness. It wasn't at all unpleasant. Looking up his body, she met his gaze, pleased to see how warm his brown eyes were. "I have never done this before, Fitzwilliam."

"I should hope not." He scowled as though the idea displeased him. Then his expression relaxed. "Just do what feels right."

Closing her eyes, Lizzy put her mouth around him, grimacing a bit at the girth. He really was large enough that she doubted her ability to engulf him completely. Patience and lots of saliva proved to be the solution, and he was soon in her mouth to the point where his head rested at the back of her tongue.

Experimentally, she twirled her

tongue around the shaft, paying attention to the way he groaned when the broad part of her tongue pressed against the underside of his cock. She focused on that area, applying pressure with her tongue that she alternated with licks. Lizzy also tried sucking him, but it was awkward with his size.

"Suck in your cheeks," he said, placing his hand at the back of her head. When she complied, he began to thrust gently in and out of her mouth, slowly pushing the limits of how deeply she could take him. "Try to relax your throat so I can go in deeper, sweetness."

Lizzy concentrated on relaxing,

doing her best not to panic at the choking sensation as he sank deeper inside her mouth. After a moment, the feeling of not being able to breathe passed, and while it wasn't exactly comfortable, she could hold him inside her throat. Cautiously, she returned to sucking him as he rocked in and out of her, fucking her face with slow strokes.

His fluid was increasing, coating her tongue and dripping down her throat. Putting a hand on his ass to steady herself, she could feel the muscles twitching underneath her skin and figured he must be getting close to coming.

Abruptly, Fitzwilliam pulled out

of her mouth and shifted to straddle her. The head of his cock probed at her cunny as he repositioned her. "I want to be inside you so badly, Lizzy."

She smiled, heart racing with excitement that she would soon lose her virginity, and to a man she had never expected. Her guardian, who would soon be her lover. "I want that too."

He looked annoyed, but she soon realized not with her. "I do not have my condom nearby. You probably do not know what that is." He shook his head, looking irritated, but not with her.

Lizzy frowned in disappointment. Wickham had

explained the device to her, assuring her it would prevent her from getting with child before their marriage, even though they were planning to begin having relations as soon as the engagement was formalized. "I do. Wickham said he would take care of me and explained what a condom is."

Fitzwilliam pushed in an inch or so, staying in her untried passage for a moment before withdrawing. "I should stop." Again, he thrust into her, going a little deeper, to the barrier of her hymen, where he froze. "That would require tearing myself away from your pretty quim." Easing out, he pushed back in again slowly, this time to her hymen and a bit beyond. The stretched, burning sensation made her shift uncomfortably, and he put his hand between them to find her clit.

As his fingers fondled her clit, she arched against him, bringing his cock a bit deeper inside her. "Maybe you could pull out at the end?"

He groaned, letting his body in a bit deeper as his fingers continued working her slick button. "That is a sound idea, Lizzy. You are quite intelligent."

"Thank you," she said, thrusting against him as his cock breached her hymen, ripping through the delicate barrier as gently as he could. It elicited a startled cry from her, but his fingers on her clit soon soothed the pain.

"God, you are tight, Lizzy." He sank deeper, taking her an inch at a time. "I have never had such a tight quim around me."

"I hope that is a good thing." She moaned as he pinched her clit and slipped in deeper.

"It is amazing, but I am afraid I might not pull out in time." Fitzwilliam bottomed out inside her, his balls pressing against her mound, and his cock stretching her quim to the point where she didn't know if she wanted to scream from pleasure, pain, or both.

"Oh, that could be a problem." It was hard to focus on any problems with Fitzwilliam's huge cock buried completely inside her. The head rested against her cervix.

"Yes." He seemed to be straining to hold back his release as he withdrew a couple of inches before slowly thrusting into her again. "What was your last monthly?"

That was an embarrassingly intimate topic, though she knew it was ridiculous to feel shy about it when they were having sex. "About two weeks ago."

He groaned. "Two weeks from

the beginning or the end?"

It took a moment to focus as he continued stroking her clit and thrusting into her, alternating shallow and deep strokes. "Um, beginning."

Fitzwilliam cursed. "Right. I have to pull out now. It is too risky." He said the words, but he didn't move. His face was red with exertion, and he seemed to be struggling with the decision.

"Oh, do not leave." She tightened her thighs around his waist, clamping him against her. The thought of him pulling out of her body before getting them both off was unbearable.

"I do not want to, sweetness,

but you could get pregnant." He cursed again. "It is way too likely, since you are young and no doubt fertile." He said the last part with a groan of pain. "I am sure your womb is ready, and there is an egg just waiting for my sperm to come along."

A growl of pleasure accompanied his next thrust into her, and he let the full length rest inside her. "If I keep going, you shall swell up with my babe inside you. Is that what you want? Do you want me to fuck a baby into you, my sweet?" The husky exhilaration tingeing his tone suggested he liked the idea a lot.

"Yes," she shouted, honestly

convinced it was the best idea ever. If the alternative was this bond ending prematurely, of having him pull away from her and never feeling this way again, she'd have her guardian's baby, even without marriage. "Fill me, Fitzwilliam. I do not care what happens tomorrow. I need you right now."

He groaned, his hand leaving her clit to slide under her ass. As he thrust in and out of her, he angled her hips a bit, so his cock hit a spot deep inside her that made her cry out and flex around him. "You are mine now, Lizzy. Always. I shall arrange for a special license, and we will be wed within the week."

"Yours," she consented, matching his thrusts as the fire burned low in her belly, spreading outward with such strength that her entire body shuddered and shook. "Make me yours, Fitzwilliam. Your wife. Your everything."

His cock convulsed inside her as her cunny clamped around him, wringing every drop of his precious cum from his prick. Her orgasm crashed over her, and tears streamed from her eyes. She sobbed his name as she came, and he gave a hoarse shout as he sank deeply inside her, spilling the last bit of his cum against her cervix, possibly giving her his baby as he soon planned to give her his name. What an incredible first time with Fitzwilliam.

www.ingramcontent.com/pod-product-compliance
Lightning Source LLC
Chambersburg PA
CBHW071425150726
48000CB00001B/479